THE PIRATE OF KINDERGARTEN

by George Ella Lyon

illustrated by Lynne Avril

A Richard Jackson Book

ATHENEUM BOOKS FOR YOUNG READERS

New York London Toronto Sydney

ATHENEUM BOOKS FOR YOUNG READERS

An imprint of Simon & Schuster Children's Publishing Division

1230 Avenue of the Americas, New York, New York 10020

For information about special discounts for bulk purchases, please contact Simon & Schuster

Special Sales at 1-866-506-1949 or business@simonandschuster.com.

The Simon & Schuster Speakers Bureau can bring authors to your live event. For more

information or to book an event, contact the Simon & Schuster Speakers Bureau at

1-866-248-3049 or visit our website at www.simonspeakers.com.

Book design by Debra Sfetsios

The text for this book is set in Adobe Garamond.

The illustrations for this book are rendered in chalk pastels mixed with

acrylic medium, and prismacolor pencils.

Manufactured in China

0110 SCP

First Edition

10 9 8 7 6 5 4 3 2 1

Library of Congress Cataloging-in-Publication Data

Lyon, George Ella, 1949–

The pirate of kindergarten / George Ella Lyon ; illustrated by Lynne Avril. — 1st ed.

p. cm.

Summary: Ginny's eyes play tricks on her, making her see everything double, but when she

goes to vision screening at school and discovers that not everyone sees this way, she learns that

her double vision can be cured.

ISBN 978-1-4169-5024-0 (hardcover)

[1. Vision—Fiction. 2. Vision disorders—Fiction. 3. Schools—Fiction.] I. Avril, Lynne,

1951– ill. II. Title.

PZ7.L9954Pi 2010

[E]—dc22

2009032113

For everyone who sees the world differently
—G. E. L.

To Wowie D. and Mackie
(and Sydney, I'm sorry I stole your glasses)
—L. A.

Ginny loved Reading Circle.

Getting there was hard, though, with all those chairs.

She knew only half of them were real, but which ones?

She always ran into some. Someone always laughed.

Ginny loved reading anyway—
from the Big Book
Ms. Cleo held in her lap . . .

or the flip chart
she pointed to with a stick . . .

or best of all
from the book Ginny held in her hands.

Ginny stuck her nose in the fold of the book.

"Ginny,"
Ms. Cleo said,
"we read with our eyes,
not our noses."

But Ginny's eyes played tricks.

She read:

Cat ran fast

She thought everyone saw this way.
She didn't know they were tricks.

When other kids laughed,
Ginny really tightened her mind
the way you tie a knot in a rope.
Then she could remember to read only
"Cat ran fast."

But after that she'd get afraid and read it again, only softer.

And then Ms. Cleo's hand
was resting on Ginny's head
    as she said, "Just once, Ginny.
We read it just once."

If Ginny closed one eye, she only saw one word, but Ms. Cleo said, "Don't squint."

Numbers hopped around like popcorn.

When she looked at the chart
or the board or the book,
she saw twice as many
2s like swans
and 3s like Bs
and big-bellied 6s

as the other kids saw.

Ginny liked their shapes.

She liked to draw them.
And she liked to color.

Scissors—scissors were tricky.

If she didn't keep her mind tied tight when Ms. Cleo gave them rabbit pictures, she might cut out one ear

Once she got so mad, she stuck the scissors in the paste.

Carl told.

Ms. Cleo said,
"A three-eared bunny! Original!"
and, "Just wash the scissors, Ginny."

This time the teacher patted Carl's hand.
"Mind your own bunnies," she said.

Then came Vision Screening Day.
Ginny was a little scared
when they lined up to go into the gym.

She did fine at first
reading letters on the white chart.
The nurse put a black spoon
over one eye and asked her to
name the letters.

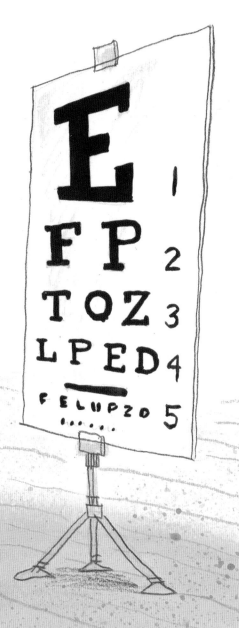

She could do that.
With one eye,
she saw only one.
It was the same
when he covered
the other eye.

But when the
nurse said, "Now
use both,"
Ginny froze.
He pointed to the
row of letters.

If they had been words, she could have read just once,

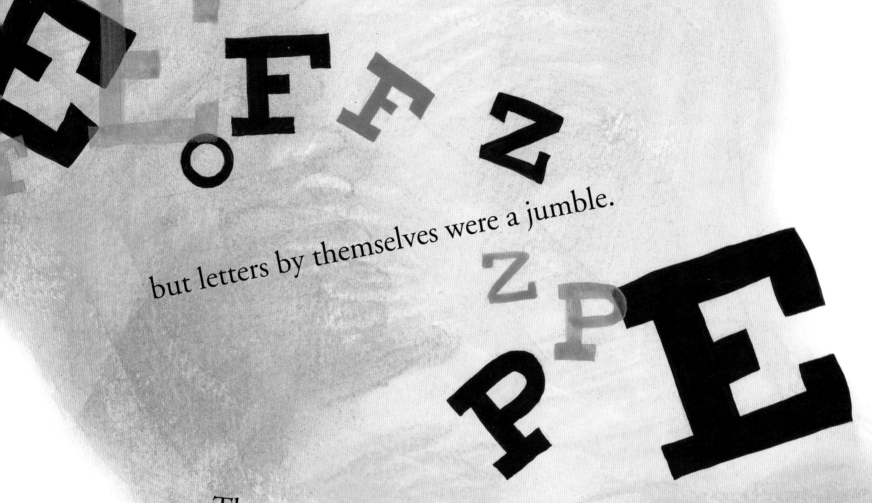

but letters by themselves were a jumble.

The nurse tapped the chart again. "This line, please."

Ginny said all she could say.
She said what she saw:

He pointed to the next line. Ginny read the same way.
The nurse's voice was gentle. "Do you see two?"
Ginny nodded.
"Do you see two of me?" he asked.
She nodded again.

"Do you know," the nurse asked, "that most people see only one?"

Ms. Cleo appeared and put a hand on Ginny's shoulder. "What's wrong?" she asked.

"This child has double vision," the nurse explained. "She needs to go to a doctor for her eyes." He looked at Ginny. "This can be fixed so you'll see only one."

The next week Ginny's mother took her to Dr. Clare.
He had Ginny look through special lenses in a dark room.
It didn't hurt, but it made her a little dizzy.

When they were finished, Dr. Clare said,
"Good news! I don't think you'll need an operation—
just exercises, glasses, and for a while, a patch."

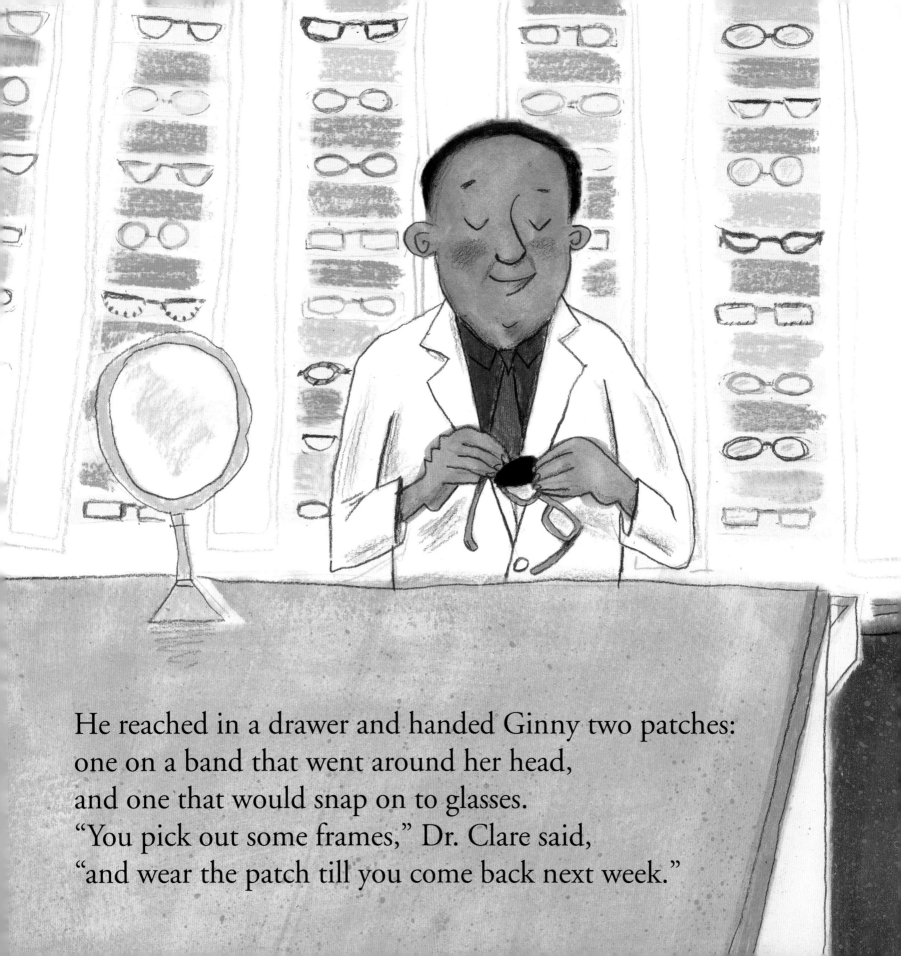

He reached in a drawer and handed Ginny two patches:
one on a band that went around her head,
and one that would snap on to glasses.
"You pick out some frames," Dr. Clare said,
"and wear the patch till you come back next week."

Ginny's mother helped her
put it on. Now there was
just *one* of everything,
and she didn't have to squint!

So Ginny became a Kindergarten Pirate

who could do numbers

and scissors,

who could climb the rigging of the playground fast . . .

and read

and read
and read.

and take her place in the Circle
without knocking over
a single chair.